THE
NEXT SURE
THING

THE
NEXT SURE
THING

RICHARD WAGAMESE

RAVEN BOOKS
an imprint of
ORCA BOOK PUBLISHERS

Library and Archives Canada Cataloguing in Publication

Wagamese, Richard.
The next sure thing / written by Richard Wagamese.
(Rapid reads)

Issued also in electronic formats.
ISBN 978-1-55469-900-1

I. Title. II. Series: Rapid reads
PS8595.A363N49 2011   C813'.54   C2011-903452-2

First published in the United States, 2011
Library of Congress Control Number: 2011929009

Summary: A young blues guitar player risks everything
when he signs on to pick winning horses at the racetrack
for a violent mobster. (RL 3.8)

*Orca Book Publishers is dedicated to preserving the environment and has
printed this book on paper certified by the Forest Stewardship Council®.*

Orca Book Publishers gratefully acknowledges the support for
its publishing programs provided by the following agencies:
the Government of Canada through the Canada Book Fund and the
Canada Council for the Arts, and the Province of British Columbia
through the BC Arts Council and the Book Publishing Tax Credit.

Design by Teresa Bubela
Cover photography by Getty Images

ORCA BOOK PUBLISHERS   ORCA BOOK PUBLISHERS
PO Box 5626, Stn. B   PO Box 468
Victoria, BC Canada   Custer, WA USA
V8R 6S4   98240-0468

www.orcabook.com
Printed and bound in Canada.

14 13 12 11 • 4 3 2 1

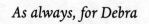

As always, for Debra

CHAPTER ONE

So I'm walking out of Shelly's Crab Shack around 2:00 AM with a handful of bills from my tip jar, and the moon is like a freaking eyeball staring right down at me. I'm tired. Sometimes these gigs are more of a hardship than a blessing. But there never was a bluesman worth his salt that didn't have to pay his dues. Me, I figure a few nights working shabby rooms like the lounge in Shelly's is gonna be worth it once I hit. I have to hit. There's no way I can't. I got me a handful of surefire riffs born from the blues I carry in my bones, man.

I was raised on a poor-as-hell Indian reservation smack-dab in the middle of nowhere, with twenty people sharing a three-bedroom house that had no glass on the windows and no electricity, and we had to haul the day's water from the lake in a five-gallon lard pail. So I know the territory of the blues. I been down so long it looks like up to me. That's how the old song goes, and I truly know how that feels. Trust me.

With a name like Cree Thunderboy, I'm a shoo-in. That's as honest a blues name as Lightnin' Hopkins, Muddy Waters or Sonny Boy Williamson. Getting folks to notice is the hard part. There's really no blues scene in this town. It's not really a working man's town. Ever since the high-tech boom, there's nothing but ISPs and systems-management joints or software-development places. And they mostly employ nerds and geeks who only listen to over-produced rock or pop or white-boy hip-hop.

I busked for over a year on the sidewalk for nickels and dimes before Shel Lashofsky stopped to check me out on his lunch hour one day. He looked at me like I mattered. Like he cared what I was playing. So I vibed him out with some slick harmonica and some down-home thumping on the bass strings of my ratty old Gibson, before peeling out a five-note run that would curdle cheese, man. That's how I got the gig at Shelly's, which is what Shel calls his place.

Trouble is, there's never anyone there. People come there to eat and head out to a shinier, more glamorous place. I wouldn't call Shel's a dump, but it's close. He serves up some good food, but he doesn't spend much on decor. Shel calls it realism. He says he's keeping it as close to Louisiana Cajun as he can even though, as far as I know, he's never been south of Ohio. So I plug in and play to six or seven people, maybe even a dozen on a good night.

But a gig is a gig, and I don't sweat the lack of big tips. In fact, I'll take this handful of bills to the track tomorrow and turn it into a whole lot more. Fast.

When I first came here, I worked as an exercise groom for one of the big horse trainers. I'd have to be up at like four o'clock to get to the track before the sun was up, but I never minded. It was like going to school. I got a diploma in picking winning horses because I'd listen to the jockeys and the trainers talk about each day's race card and whose horses were right and whose weren't. I learned how to tell when a horse is ready just by looking at it. But you can't bet when you work the back lot, so I quit after six months. After that I just bet.

The only trouble with that was that the track got successful. Pretty soon there were new and bigger trainers with whole stables of horses I didn't know. There were a lot of new jockeys. So I was lost. I'd been winning for a while, but this new flood of activity left me high and dry. Even though I don't win a lot, I hit often enough to keep me going back.

My dad would say it's the lazy man's way. He was church-raised, a real Bible-thumper. And he didn't look kindly on either gambling or playing music. But the big bluesmen, the ones who left their mark, were all about playing the blues until the wee hours of the morning. When you do that like I do now, you get up late. It's hard to make an honest job when you don't get up until noon. Besides, to be a great blues player you have to be authentic, and this life I live gives me enough grit and hard times to make my music real.

Moms Mahood doesn't mind. Moms runs the rooming house where I live. It's not much. I got the only room with a small balcony overlooking the backyard, and I sit out there and play on evenings I'm not booked. All Moms cares about is if I have the rent come the end of the week. I've been late a few times, but I'm always good for it.

I'm twenty-three years old. I don't have a girlfriend. I don't own a car. But I can play a guitar that'll shuck the husk right off a cob of corn from fifty feet away. I'm going to be a bluesman. They're gonna say my name right along with John Lee Hooker and Howlin' Wolf and Stevie Ray Vaughan. That's my dream.

I'm going to win big money at the track too. That's my other dream. Because there's always a sure thing hiding in the numbers on the racing form. I don't know if that's true or not. I just choose to believe it.

CHAPTER TWO

So there's this filly running in the third race named Ocean's Folly. I keep staring from my race form to the tote board. I can't believe my luck. No one is putting any money on this horse, and her odds are sitting at thirty to one. That's a sixty-dollar payout on a two-dollar bet. When I check the numbers, I get excited. She's only run a few times, and from the looks of things, she's what a casual fan would call a "flier and die-er." In three of her four races she's run at the front, then fallen off coming around the last turn. But she has great early speed.

Now she's in a race with veteran horses, and not one of them is a nag. All of them have speed. The race is a mile long, and she's placed in the fifth position coming out of the gate. It gives her lots of room to move. According to the tote board, everyone seems to be choosing the favorite, a big roan gelding called Majestic Image. He's won three races over the last year at this same level of competition.

But what I see in the numbers is a young, fast horse trained for this distance. You could almost write off Ocean's Folly's first few races as training runs. She's just run to build up her familiarity with the distance. No other horse can match her for pure blazing speed out of the gate. As I scan each of her races, I see that she's been stretching that speed out. Now I see that the trainer and the jockey will let her have her head in the back stretch, and it'll be up to the field to try and catch her.

I'm so excited that my legs are bouncing up and down. The tote board numbers don't change on her. I have twelve dollars in tip money left after paying admission, buying a racing form and a program. Even if I only bet ten bucks, that's over three hundred dollars if she wins. I can't believe my luck.

"Got a hot one, do you?"

I look up, and there's a big, beefy white guy looking at me and smiling. He's got one leg crossed over the other and one arm across the back of the seat. The ring on his finger has to be worth a few grand. He's dressed to kill in a white linen suit and designer shoes.

"Nah," I say. "Not really. This one's pretty set with Majestic Image."

He nods. "Hard to go against his record. There's no cabbage in the action though. Odds are too low. Who do you like?"

"No one really."

"That's not what your legs say." He gives me a level look that I have to turn away from. His eyes are piercing. He stands and moves to sit beside me and offers his hand. "Win Hardy," he says.

"Win?" I ask.

"Short for Winslow. Never took much to that. Win feels better."

"Cree," I say, shaking his hand. "Cree Thunderboy."

He laughs. "Now that's a handle and a half. So who do you like, Mr. Thunderboy?"

"Maybe the nine horse. The odds are long, but in this kinda race you have to go that way to make anything."

"You always bet to win?"

"Don't you?"

"Sometimes," he says and smiles. His teeth are dazzling. "Sometimes I just bet to learn."

"Expensive lessons."

"Maybe. But you can't put a dollar value on knowledge."

"What is it you hope to learn?" I'm not normally this open with strangers, but this guy just sort of oozes charm, and I can't help myself.

"People."

"Excuse me?"

He laughs. It's a low rumbling kind of laugh, manly and strong, and I like it.

"I like to learn people. I study them. I watch how they play, how they scrutinize, how they react to information. Like your leg. You were composed for a long time, and then the more you read, the more your leg got a life of its own. It's your tell."

"My tell?"

"Yeah. Like in poker. Everyone's got a tell, a subtle little sign when they sense a winner or get nervous."

"What's yours?"

He laughs again, sits straighter in his seat and looks out at the tote board. When he looks at me again, his face is blank as a stone. "I don't have one."

"I thought you said everyone did."

"Everyone but me, I meant. I never get nervous."

It was my turn to laugh, and when I did, he laughed too.

"Everyone gets nervous when it comes to money," I said. "Nervous to win and nervous to lose. It's your last bottom dollar that'll give you the blues."

"What is that, a poem?"

"Nah. It's a lyric. From one of my songs."

"Really? A songwriter? The blues, I'm guessing."

"You'd guess right then."

"Well, isn't that amazing."

"How so?"

He hands me a business card from an alligator-skin wallet. There's at least half an inch of money tucked in there. The card features a metal-flake comet in the top corner and says *Win Hardy Talent Management*. The card stock feels hefty, assured, confident.

"You're a talent agent?"

"Well, let's just say I have an interest in people that can make me money."

"At the track?"

"I've found that talent isn't limited to a specific area."

"What does that mean exactly?"

"It means if you tell me who you like in this race and convince me to like them too, I'll add to the ten bucks you've got to bet with."

"How do you know that ten bucks is all I have to bet with?"

He smiled again. "Well, for one thing, you just told me. For another, you're a blues

13

player in a town with no blues scene, so you're not gigging much. Lastly, you have the look of someone looking for one good hit, not someone out at the track for an enjoyable afternoon in the sunshine."

"But you'd throw in with me if I tell you about this horse?"

He laughed and clapped me soundly on the back. It felt good. It felt all buddy-buddy and masculine. "See, I knew you had a line on something. So if it's not Majestic Image, who is it?"

I wound up telling him everything, and for some reason it didn't really surprise me.

CHAPTER THREE

He gave me twenty dollars, and when Ocean's Folly won by three-quarters of a length over Majestic Image, I collected almost nine hundred dollars. He did better than me. He won enough that they had to pay him by check. The first thing I did was pay him back the twenty. He studied me a moment, nodded, pocketed the money and led me upstairs to the clubhouse, where we sat on plush seats while a waiter served us drinks.

He sat back in his chair like a king. He spread both arms out over the backs of the adjacent seats and puffed on a long Cuban cigar. He had the expensive look of a Cadillac fresh off the lot. When he drank, he held the glass with a thumb and two fingers, and I thought it was a very delicate move for such a large man.

I watched people watch him. He had a way of drawing their eyes. It wasn't in any way I could determine. He just drew people. They couldn't stop looking at him. The men eyed him with envy, and the women offered coy looks over the tops of their programs or the rim of their drink glasses. I felt proud to be sitting with him.

"Well, Mr. Cree Thunderboy," he said. "That was very nice. Thrilling, even. You got any more aces up your sleeve?"

"Nothing that steps up and asks me to dance."

He laughed and waved at the waiter for fresh drinks. I never drank scotch. In fact, I hardly drank at all. It was the one bluesman thing I could never get a fond-ness for. I liked being clear. But the stuff he was buying was smooth and warm and smoky-tasting, and I liked it.

"Come on. You got the touch, kid. I can tell. Who do you like in the fifth?"

I shook my head. "No one."

"Come on."

"No. All the way up to the tenth, there's nothing. Sure things don't come around all that often. Most people think there's one in every box, as if life is like Cracker Jacks. It's not. You got to ride a lot of rail before the train hits the station again."

"You mix your metaphors. But I get you. You're saying, take the money and run. Grin all the way to the bank."

"I suppose. I never had a lot of loot in my time. So I tend to treat it carefully."

"Wise," he said. "I wonder, though, what you would do if you had a lot of loot, as you say?"

"That's not a bridge I'm likely to cross anytime soon."

"You tend to talk like a song lyric, do you know that?"

I laughed. "Comes with the territory, I guess."

"Yeah, well, if you stick with me, you might not be singing the blues too long. I can use a bright kid like you."

"I'm not a kid."

He turned and fixed me with that blank unreadable look again. The scotch left me able to hold it.

"You're right," he said. "You're not. I apologize. Figure of speech is all. I sometimes have too much of a Humphrey Bogart fixation."

"It's all right," I said. "But what do you mean, if I stick with you?"

"Well, Cree, I'm in the business of making money. I hire people who can do that for me. People with a talent. People with

18

a dream. They work for me and use their talent, and I make their dreams come true."

"You've never even heard me play."

"No, but you know how to pick a winner. That's the talent I want. You do that for me, and I'll get you into a recording studio and promote your music. Hell, I'll even ante up for a video. The whole works. You just need to make your other talent available to me."

"For how long?"

He reached out an arm and clenched me around the shoulders. I could feel the bulk of his muscles and the strength of him. "Time is relative where loot is concerned."

"You can actually do all that? Recording, videos?"

"I have certain friends who can make certain things happen."

"There's no way I can find you a winner every day."

"Maybe not. But you do it often enough, like you just did today, and I'd be a happy man, and my friends would be too. Everyone likes the easy money. Keeps things simple."

It made me uncomfortable. Still, the idea of actually getting into a recording studio and making the album I'd always dreamed of was too hard to resist. His confidence was magnetic. "So what do I do?" I asked.

"You get the form, you make your pick, you come down here, check out the animal, and if it looks good, you go."

"With what? I'm a ten-dollar bettor."

He reached into his wallet and handed me a quarter inch of hundred-dollar bills. "Let's just call this an advance on your commissions. Your grub stake. You work the sheet tonight. Call me. I get the money to you. You come here, make the bet and bring me the winnings. Easy."

"How do I reach you?"

"The number's on the card. And here's a phone." He reached into his jacket pocket and handed me a small cell phone. "The number's speed-listed. Just press *One*."

"You carry phones to give away to people?"

"They're phones for my talent. I'm telling you, Cree, I take care of details. You take care of your end, I'll have you out on CD in no time."

"Sounds too easy."

He laughed. "The best things always are. And what you said about sure things? Sometimes they just walk right up and introduce themselves."

CHAPTER FOUR

Ashton Crooker is my best friend. He used to bring his djembe drum and give me rhythm backup while I played on the street. The funny thing about that is we never talked the first three times. He'd just show up, drum behind me and leave. He never asked for any of the tips. It always seemed like he found joy in the playing and that was all he wanted.

So one rainy day when there wasn't a lot of action, we headed for a coffee joint to warm up. We found out that we shared a passion for music. Ashton liked all kinds and filled my ears with talk of African, Brazilian and Cuban bands and drummers I should hear. We'd sit around his bachelor apartment and listen to music and talk long into the night sometimes. I told him about my life on the reservation and how the blues just reached out and touched me. He told me about growing up poor in a trailer park on the outskirts of Montreal and how drumming always seemed to make him feel better. He said he could even drum away hunger. That was the power of music. We were friends after that.

Now we sat in the same coffee joint, and he looked at me wide-eyed. "So he just gave you all this money?"

"Yeah. Just over three thousand."

"Commission?"

"That's what he said. An advance."

"That's too radical to be real." Ashton studied the card Hardy had given me.

"Did you even call this number? See if it's a real office?"

"No. Why would I? The guy just wants fast money. Who doesn't? I mean, if I met a guy like me and figured he could get me some easy winnings, I'd go for it too."

"You'd hand off three grand to a stranger?"

"Well, maybe not that. But it shows he's got money. Guys with that kind of money have connections, and he said he'd get me a recording session."

"I'd be careful about who his connections were."

"You know what, Ash? I don't even care. If it gets me into a studio, that's all I want."

"Yeah, but nobody's real name is Win."

I riffled the edges of the bills. "I won this."

"Maybe so," Ashton said with a worried look. "But guys like you and me, Cree, we don't get breaks like this. Not this easy.

We're working-class guys who play a little music. Dream, yeah. But stay real, buddy. Stay real."

Just then the door opened, and two very large men walked in. They had heads the size of basketballs and eyes that stared straight ahead, unreadable like the eyes of dolls. They strode right over to our table and stood there looking down at us. I was suddenly very scared.

"Which one of you is Thunderboy?" the biggest one asked.

His friend punched him in the shoulder. "Well, gee, Vic. Would it be the Indian guy or the pasty-faced white guy? Hmmm. I wonder."

"Yeah, yeah, yeah," the one named Vic said. "Mr. Hardy asks that you sign these papers." He held out a sheaf of legal-sized papers to me.

"What are they?" I said. "And how did you know where to find me?"

"Personal services agreement. Standard talent stuff," the other one said. "And we can always find you. Trust me."

Ashton and I exchanged a look. "Can I read them over?"

"I told you, standard stuff. You agreed in principle when you took the advance. So just sign the papers. We got work to do."

"What kind of work?" Ashton asked.

"Tell him, Vic."

Vic straightened up and stood as tall as he could and cast a sweeping look around the café. Then he leaned forward, his full weight on his arms. We could feel the tabletop bend. He looked right at Ashton with those bright, depthless eyes.

"Me and Jerry are commission agents. Thunderboy here pays us, we pay him. We get to be friends, have a few drinks. Maybe take in a ball game now and then. He don't pay us, the story takes a slightly different tack. You get my drift?"

"I get it," Ashton said. "I get it." He slid back in his chair.

I signed the papers and handed them to Jerry, who folded them without looking. He put his hands in his pants pockets, and his coat flapped back to reveal the butt of a gun in his belt. We stared at it. Hard. When we looked up at him, he was grinning.

"Sometimes things get tough in the commission business. We wouldn't want that to happen to you, Wonderboy."

"That's Thunderboy," I said.

"Same difference from what I hear. Be ready at nine AM. We'll pick you up."

"For what?"

Jerry slapped Vic playfully on the back, and the bigger man curled up his fists and ducked his head and shoulders down in a boxer's shuffle step.

"For what, the kid asks."

"Dumb kid," Vic said and stood beside Jerry. "You signed the deal. You should know the play. We pick you up in the morning and deliver you to the studio, where you cut some tracks. I hear you're some kind of whiz kid on guitar."

"I'm recording? Just like that?"

"Just like that, like it says in the deal," Vic said. "Then in the afternoon we deliver you to the track and you do your thing for the boss man. Here's tomorrow's form."

He laid the racing form on the table. Ashton and I both stared at it without moving. This all seemed to be happening very fast. The two large men watched us. When we didn't offer a response, they turned and walked toward the door. Then Vic turned on one heel and marched back, irritated.

"Don't forget to do your homework. The man needs your call before we pick you up. Got it?" he asked.

"I got it." I said. "I got it."

Ashton and I looked at each other a long time without speaking.

CHAPTER FIVE

Moms met me at the door when I got home. She was the next thing to giddy. I'd never seen her so happy. When I walked through the door, she hugged me, and I could feel her shaking.

"Are you okay?" I asked.

"More than okay," she said and stepped back to look at me. "It's so amazing what something like a little prayer can do."

"What do you mean?"

"I mean my sister has been off work for a year after her hip operation. Things weren't looking very good, and she really needed money just to get by while she was off her feet. This place keeps me going, but it doesn't give me extra to pass around. But I prayed and asked for a way to help. And the next thing you know, your boss, Mr. Hardy, shows up and pays a whole year in advance."

"He did that?" Things were happening too fast.

"Yes. He just left a half hour ago."

The cell phone in my pocket rang, and I walked out onto the porch to take the call.

"I take it you're home by now." There was a touch of a laugh in Hardy's voice.

"How did you know where I live?"

"I'm the kind of guy who likes to know everything about the people he hires."

"That's not an answer."

"It is in my book."

"Not in mine," I said.

"Well, the thing is, Cree, you're not writing the book. I am. You're walking around with a fistful of my green. And you got a date to lay down some tracks in a studio just like you always wanted to do. What's with the attitude?"

"I don't like being followed."

"No one's following you. I just like to know where my money's walking to when it walks out the door."

"Are you happy now?"

"Extremely. Nice lady, that landlady of yours. Seemed happy to have a little extra to work with. Glad I could help."

"I didn't ask you to pay my rent."

"No need. I'm your new BFF."

"Best friend forever?" I asked, irritated.

"Best friend with firearms. Just remember that." The phone went dead in my hand.

I sat in my room mulling over the events. Suddenly I didn't like Hardy much. Beyond the charm and the dazzle was a coldness that worried me. His henchmen were buffoons, but there was a hard ugliness behind their playful natures. Still, the roll of bills felt good in my hand.

My guitar and small amplifier stood in the corner, and the idea of finally making it into a recording studio excited me. But there was pressure I didn't need. The odds of finding a sure thing were long enough without the added weight of having to keep Hardy happy and avoid the dark side of his goons. I didn't like owing him. I didn't like feeling kept like a dog on a leash. I didn't like the threat hanging over me.

But the blues is built of stories of men who make deals with the devil. And the glitter of promise I saw outweighed the bad feelings in the end. I unfolded the racing form and lay back on my bed to study it. At least I got to play with my strong suit.

There wasn't a lot of action the next day. As hard as I studied, nothing emerged that smelled anything like a winner.

At least, not in the big way of Ocean's Folly. People never seem to realize that winning big takes a lot more than just knowing what to look for in the racing line. You need to know the variables. What a horse looks like by the numbers has little to do with how they look in the post parade. There's taping and liniment, the way they move, the set of their ears, if they're wearing blinders. Even the condition of the track and the weather make a difference. The numbers only get you so far, and the way they read, there was nothing to really move on.

After three hours, there was only one thing to do. There was a horse in the seventh named Sports Day, and he was listed as a five-to-one shot. That would pay a mere ten dollars on a two-dollar bet. But if a guy were to lay down a thousand, it would mean a payout of five thousand. The trouble was that Sports Day was going up in class. It meant that he would be racing stronger, more experienced horses. But his workout times impressed me, and the race was a sprint. Six furlongs. He'd raced at a mile at the lower levels and always been very quick in the first half mile. It was worth a shot, if a guy had an extra thousand to lay down. I did, but the idea made me nervous.

This was no sure thing. It was a risk. Hardy wanted bets that would cash out, and there was no way of knowing whether this one would make the cut. I decided that I would use some of the advance money and make the bet myself. I'd tell Hardy there was nothing going on the race card that day. I could learn something betting big money and not have to risk losing Hardy's cash and maybe not being able to record my songs. That was the most important thing. When you get this close to a dream, you can't let it go. You can't.

I told myself that move was all about education. I told myself it was preparing me for doing what Hardy wanted me to do. I told myself it was okay. Still, I didn't sleep much that night. Playing big money will do that to you.

CHAPTER SIX

The recording engineer was a guy named Keys. They called him that because he'd been a hot keyboard player when he was young and had actually toured with some big-name jazz groups. But he developed arthritis in his hands. Keys knew his way around a soundboard though. And he knew how to talk to musicians and how they liked to work. I felt comfortable right away. He set me up behind some wooden sound baffles with a stool and a microphone and my guitar plugged into an old Fender tube amp.

He said it would give my riffs a good old-time sound. It did.

We laid down five songs that morning. I'd only ever heard myself on cheap tape recorders before. The way the studio recording sounded made me feel ten feet tall. The guitar runs were crystal clear, and when I vamped the chords, they were all fat and thumpy like the old-time bluesmen. My voice sounded raspy and growly and very blue.

"We got something here," Keys said. "It's bluesy, jazzy, very funky. I like it. You write good stuff."

I'd never felt prouder.

Vic and Jerry hung around for the whole session. They hadn't been too happy when I told them there was nothing to bet that day. They were less impressed when I booked out of there alone.

"The boss won't like this much," Vic said. "Things are a little one-ended here."

"Well, what would you have me do? Lie to him? Lay down dumb money just so he's happy knowing there's action?"

"Maybe not. But you have to give him the word. Not me."

Vic punched in some numbers and then handed me the phone. Hardy answered right away.

"Yeah," was all he said.

"It's me. Cree."

"Hey, Wonderboy. How's the action looking?"

"Well, if it was my money, I'd keep it in my pocket today."

"Why?"

"There's nothing. Everything's a toss-up. I wouldn't put your cash out there."

"You're not just saying that?"

"No."

There was a silence at the end of the line. Vic and Jerry eyed me. I shifted from foot to foot, waiting.

"Okay," he said finally. "You're the man. I trust you. Take the day. Spend some loot. Have a little fun. I'll talk to you later."

I handed Vic the phone, and he mumbled into it. Then broke the connection and shrugged.

"Guess you can go," he said.

"With your permission," I said.

"Don't get cute, kid. Ever."

I took that as my cue to leave.

* * *

Ashton wasn't exactly impressed with my thinking. He sat there while I told him my plan and shook his head slowly. Then he looked up at me and stared for long enough to make me nervous.

"This guy sounds like trouble if things don't follow his line," he said finally.

"I know that. But the thing is, Ash, I gotta show him that I know how to think too. Right now he's making all the moves and taking control. I don't want him thinking I'm just a flunky."

"Okay, but are you prepared to handle it if he flips out because you acted on your own?"

"He asks me to act on my own."

"To pick the horses, yeah. Not to venture out without telling him."

"I don't see the problem."

"You won't until after." He picked up his coffee and took a long slow sip. "But I'm still gonna go with you."

"Why?"

He laughed. "I've never seen anyone lay down a thousand bucks on a bet before. Nor have I watched anyone have to watch their money run around a track."

"Glad I entertain you."

By the time we got to the track, the grandstand was full. We'd missed the first four races, and the action for the fifth was fast and heavy, according to the numbers on the tote board. We picked up some burgers, Cokes and a racing form and found a quiet area that overlooked the paddock area so we could see the horses when they arrived prior to their race. Ashton liked to people-watch. He sat and ate and looked over the crowd while I thumbed through the form. I was so nervous that I had trouble reading. Finally I put the form down and ate my burger while I watched the horses and jockeys get ready in the paddock. Just for something to do, I walked to the window and put a ten-dollar bet on a big roan gelding called Falmouth's Boy. I never made pointless bets, but I was antsy. I needed a distraction. Ashton followed my lead and bet five dollars on the same horse. He won by half a head.

"How'd you know?" Ashton asked as we cashed out.

"I guessed," I said.

"Good guess."

"Yeah. But I never do that. It's being foolish."

"Foolishness just made me fifteen bucks."

"Yeah, well, luck is luck, I guess."

"Hope your luck holds out in the seventh."

We killed time until the horses paraded for the seventh and I got a chance to look at Sports Day. He was muscular and fit-looking but smaller than the rest of the field. There was a knot of anxiety in my gut. I fingered the roll of bills in my pocket and toyed with the idea of just forgetting it and waiting until I could find a sure thing for Hardy. But I needed to show him that I was independent, that I could operate on my own. I didn't like feeling owned. This was my chance to gain a little freedom. With three minutes to post time, I walked up and made the bet. My hands shook while I counted out the bills. My mouth was dry, and I gulped down a Coke. There was no way I could sit to watch the race, so we stood at the rail at the edge of the second-floor seats. Ashton watched me worriedly.

"You gonna be okay?"

"I hope so."

When the horses charged out of the starting gate, Sports Day was almost invisible behind the larger horses. But his size let him slip between them, and he found daylight. The gate was at the foot of the backstretch, and I could see him race into the far turn, leading by half a length. I thought I would faint. He led through the turn, and then a pair of bigger horses made a move and drew even with his shoulder. Down the homestretch, there wasn't an inch to separate them. Every lunging stride seemed to push one of the three ahead. The crowd was wild. I leaned on the railing and clutched it hard.

Time slowed. Everything seemed to move in slow motion. I could hear Ashton yelling in my ear, but the words didn't register. My hands hurt from gripping the rail.

When the horses flashed across the finish line, Sports Day had won by a nose. I wobbled to a seat and flopped down in it. I could barely breathe. I put my head on my forearms and swallowed huge gulps of air. When I looked up, Ashton was smiling at me.

"You just won five thousand dollars," he said.

I still hadn't got my breath back when we returned to the counter for the winnings.

CHAPTER SEVEN

You walk a little different when you carry a check for five grand in your wallet. There's a casual flow to your stride and you feel like walking is easier. You feel light-headed and you breathe shallower. And if you close your eyes, you get the feeling that you might just float away. That's how I felt as Ashton and I walked away from the racetrack. I'd never won so much before. But then, I had never bet so much either. My nerves were frayed and I was still jittery. But I was full of energy—vibrating, really. I wouldn't have changed those feelings for anything.

"That was freakin' awesome," Ashton said. "Thrilling, scary, wonderful all at the same time."

"I thought I was going to lose it at the end," I said.

"Jeez. He only won because he exhaled when the other horses inhaled. That's how close it was."

"Tell me about it." I was still lost in the thrill of the race and that heady feeling that comes when you're so excited you forget to breathe.

The day was suddenly sunnier and warmer than it had been before. I laughed and punched Ashton on the shoulder. He winced and grabbed at it, but he laughed too. We walked faster toward the bus stop. We were shaking our heads and talking about what we'd do with the rest of the day when a black Lincoln Navigator swung in across the sidewalk in front of us. Neither of us was too surprised when Vic and Jerry stepped out.

"Both of you. In the back," Jerry said. His hand was in the front of his blazer.

Ashton was pale. I looked at Vic, and he just shook his head at me and held out one hand to the open back door of the suv. We climbed in. The silence was hard. Neither of them spoke at all. Vic drove, and Jerry sat staring straight ahead. Ashton and I fidgeted nervously while we made our way through downtown traffic. Finally we pulled up behind a long red-brick warehouse.

"Get out," was all Jerry said.

They walked us in the back door. It looked like an auto parts place. There were long rows of shelving where workers were gathering items and boxing them to place on conveyors that carried them to other workers, who loaded them onto trucks at a pair of loading docks. No one bothered to look at us as we passed. We were marched up a set of stairs and through a set of offices with secretaries busy with paperwork. The silence was the worst. Neither Vic nor Jerry spoke all that time. They just walked solemnly behind us. We could feel the weight of their big bodies following us, and we walked as fast as we could. We ended up in a paneled office with floor-to-ceiling windows overlooking the street. Vic motioned us to sit on a leather couch along one wall. They went to stand at either side of the door.

Hardy entered through a side door. He walked to his desk without looking at us or speaking. When he sat, he drank from a tumbler and eyed me over the rim. Then he put it on the table softly—so gently it gave me the creeps. He folded his hands in front of him and leaned forward in his chair.

"Never did much care for freelancers, Cree. I expected some degree of loyalty from you." He leaned back in his chair.

"I don't know what you mean," I said.

"You took my money and made your own play. You left me out of the loop. I call that a total lack of respect."

"That's not what happened."

He stood up suddenly. He leveled a hard look at me.

"You take a grand of my money and put it to work and you don't tell me about it? You pick up five grand, and you're gonna walk off and play like nothing happened? Like you didn't use my generosity for your own end? Don't play me, Cree. We know what you did."

"You had me followed?"

"You think I don't have people at the track? I knew as soon as you got there, and I knew when you made your play. Nice trick though. Waiting until just before the bell went off to lay down your wager. Makes it hard for anyone else to get in."

"I waited because it took me that long to be sure."

"Sure of what? That you were in the clear?"

"No," I said and stood up too. Vic and Jerry took a half-step forward. "To be sure that it was the right move."

"It wasn't," Hardy said. "You used my money. You cheated me."

"Our deal was for me to let you know when there was a sure thing," I said. "This wasn't. This could have gone totally the other way." I looked at the goons. They spread their legs wider and clasped their hands in front of themselves and rocked on the balls of their feet. "I didn't tell you because I didn't want you to risk your money. So I used the cash you gave me because you said it was mine. That way if I lost, it was my loss. I didn't think you thought it was still yours."

"You still made a play without telling me. Disobedience doesn't earn you any points, Cree. It just earns you pain.

51

Or it earns your friend pain." He nodded to Vic, and the big guy reached over and hauled Ashton to his feet by the scruff of his neck. There was a large knife in his hand. Ashton looked ready to faint. Vic held the knife to his ribs and looked at Hardy.

"Ever wonder why they use the term 'blood money,' Cree?" Hardy asked.

"No," I said nervously.

"Because it's earned by blood. Your pal's blood, unfortunately. You want to mess with me? This is how you pay for that."

"Why?" I said and took a step forward. I heard Jerry move with me. "Because I took a risk without involving you? Because that risk paid out? Because I took a counter check from the track with your name on it?"

Hardy looked stunned. "What did you say?"

"You heard me. The check's made out to you."

"You kidding me?"

"Look for yourself." I held the paper out, and Hardy stepped around the desk and took it.

"Well, damned if it isn't," he said.

"I know about loyalty," I said. "You got me into a studio where I laid down five tracks for an album. You gave me the first installment on my dream, and I took this risk because it wasn't a sure thing. I thought you gave me that money without strings. I didn't want to risk your cash. This way if I lost, it was my loss, not yours. That's what I figured."

Hardy smiled. "I knew you were a good kid."

He reached out and shook my hand. He held on to it tightly and looked over my shoulder and nodded at Vic, and I could hear Ashton collapse onto the couch.

"But don't ever make a move without telling me again," he said. "Not even a small one. If you know about loyalty, you'll take care of your friend."

All I could do was nod.

CHAPTER EIGHT

We sat at a small sidewalk café. Ashton, Hardy and me. Vic and Jerry sat in the Navigator a few yards down the street. It was warm in the late afternoon. The café was filled with people chatting and laughing. There were plates of appetizers in front of us and glasses of good white wine. But neither Ashton nor I were much in the mood for food or drink. Hardy ate triumphantly. He eyed me over his fork, then set it down and wiped at the corner of his mouth with a napkin.

"I got friends that want to meet you," he said.

"I have friends," I said.

"Not like these. These are friends that can make your world. Or break it just as easily."

"Why would I want to meet people like that?"

He smiled and drank some wine. "Mostly because you don't have a choice. See, I work for these guys, and they're interested in your talent too. While you were waiting for me in the car, I told them about your five-to-one shot and how you played it. They like your moxie."

"Moxie?"

"Yeah. Balls. You know."

"I don't."

"Everyone gets scared, Cree. The trouble is that most people don't move through it. It cripples them. Not you. You push through it. Even if you piss people off. That's moxie, and my friends want it working for them."

"I don't work for anybody."

Hardy spun his wineglass slowly in his fingers. "You work for me."

"I thought we had a deal."

"The deal is you work for me. And you work for my friends. That should be clear by now."

"I think I want out."

Hardy laughed then. It was genuine. As though no one had ever told him quite as big a joke before. He fumbled in his coat for his cell phone and punched in a number on speed dial.

"Kid says he wants out," he said into it and smiled at me and shook his head. "That's what I did too. Cracked me right up. Hey, he's a green kid, never done nothing in his life. What do you expect?" He listened for a moment and a deep line appeared in between his eyebrows. He nodded, then looked at Ashton and handed him the phone.

"Guess you get to translate, buddy boy. My friend would like to speak to you."

"Me? Why?"

Hardy chuckled. "Ask him."

Ashton gave me a quizzical look and held the phone up to his ear.

"Yes?" he said.

I watched his face change. It went from curious to worried to shocked right in front of me. He held the phone so tightly that his knuckles went white, and he breathed through his mouth like a kid. I could hear a thin seam of voice from the phone. It was regular, straight, without rises or changes in pitch or volume. Ashton just listened, and when he handed the phone back to Hardy, he couldn't look at me.

"Tell him," was all Hardy said. He said it coldly. Ashton stared at him a moment before turning to me.

When Ashton looked at me, his face looked like he'd been slapped. It was white and strained.

"Leo Scalia," he said.

"Excuse me?" I said.

"Leo Scalia," Ashton said again, more urgently. "Hardy works for Leo Scalia. He runs book for the mob. Hardy's connected. He's made. You can't quit."

I looked at Hardy, who sat back in his chair with his legs crossed, grinning at me. "You're connected?"

"Big-time," he said. "But hey, my friends are your friends, Cree. You're our pony now. Or at least, you're mine. Quitting? Well, no one likes a quitter, do they?"

"I can't do this," I said.

"Can't do what? We're only asking you to do what you already know how to do. This is no stretch. Hell, if you want, you don't even have to carry any action.

You don't have to make the bets. You just make the tote, give us the number. We play the horse, and you get your commission and our endless high regard. Besides, I own the paper on your whole friggin' life. So what's 'can't do'?"

"What are you talking about?" Ashton was shaking his head beside me. Hardy waved a hand in the air. I heard the doors of the Navigator slam and the footfalls of Vic and Jerry. Hardy stood and shrugged and straightened his jacket with both hands. Then he leaned forward on the table toward me. His eyes were hard. I could smell cigar smoke and wine. He put one knuckle under my chin and lifted my head. I heard the goons step up behind me.

"Call me your proud new papa, Cree. I paid your rent. I'm footing the bill for your first CD and video. You want new gear? You got that too, because I got you a gig at the Purple Onion starting next week.

You'll need a bigger amp, and me, I figure the blues sounds best on a Gretsch semi-hollow body with a nice stack of Fender amps behind it. Red, maybe. I like red. What you think, Jerry?"

"Red is good, Win. Real good," Jerry said from behind me.

"And if you do ever decide to get cute, Cree? Call your folks on the rez. Ask 'em how they like the new truck. Ask your sister how she likes having her tuition paid for. I own all of them. Not just you. So your moves are their moves now. Remember that next time you think you can quit on me. Vic? Give him tomorrow's form."

He let my chin go, grinned at me and gave me a light playful slap on the cheek.

"He's a good kid. Green, but good," he said to Vic and Jerry. Then he turned and walked away.

Ashton and I sat there in silence. I was stunned. "Can it get any worse?" I asked.

"Yeah," Ashton said. "It can."

"How's that?"

"I didn't tell you what else he does for Scalia."

I looked at him. He looked sad and scared. "Are you kidding me?"

"No," he said. "He's a collector. A knee-breaker."

I suddenly felt like drinking the wine. All of it.

CHAPTER NINE

As it turned out, Hardy's people had been to the reservation. They'd arrived in a row of three black suvs and made a big display of friendship. My family was told that Hardy was my boss and that I was working as an investment counselor. I was doing such a bang-up job that he wanted to reward me as much as he could, and helping to take care of my family was the way he had chosen. Somehow he talked the chief and his councilors into giving my family a house of their own. He furnished it too, as well as parking a new half-ton pickup truck in the driveway. All of this was fine with my father. When I'd walked away to pursue the vague dream of being a blues musician, he hadn't been thrilled. But with the arrival of Hardy's people and the outlay of goodwill cash, he seemed more willing to believe that I was actually worth something in the world.

"You work hard for this man," he said over the telephone. "He can obviously do a lot for you."

I couldn't tell him what the real score was. He had the new house, the truck and furniture, and my sister had her tuition paid for at the college where she was studying nursing.

"They left a thousand dollars that they said you would earn back in no time too," my father said. "That kind of man is someone you hold on to. Anyone can see that."

Ashton just looked at me blankly when I told him later at the coffee joint.

He hadn't said much since the encounter with Hardy and the knife at his ribs. I was worried about our friendship.

"There's got to be a way to get out from under all this," he said. "I just don't know what it is."

"I'm sorry, Ash," I said.

He shook his head.

"It wasn't your fault. These guys look for people to trap all the time. They don't have the skill set or the brains to do anything themselves. How were you to know the guy was bad?"

"I should have been more careful."

"You were doing what you do. There was never any inkling that it would go sour."

"Well, it has. Now he has my family in his pocket. They all figure he's the best thing that ever happened to me. But what scares me is how much he knows about my life and how much of it he controls now."

"He's got your back to the wall. What bothers me is the threat."

"Yeah. Everything I do, win or lose, means someone close to me will get hurt."

"Or killed," Ashton said. "They're talking big money here now. Leo Scalia doesn't play around."

"So what do I do?"

"Make your record. Make your bets. Hope for the best."

"Hope for the best?"

"I guess. There's no way out that I can see."

"How big is Scalia?"

"He's the biggest player in this town. I don't think he's got much reach beyond that, but he has his fingers in a lot of pies. There are a lot of people who only move when he lets them move."

"Like me?"

"Like you."

"For now."

He looked at me, and I could feel him searching me for a clue to what I was thinking. The truth is, I didn't really know for sure what I was thinking. I only knew that this wasn't the way the dream was supposed to go. As thrilled as I was about being able to record my album and the plans for shooting a video to put up on YouTube and maybe attract some attention from the big boys in the music biz, I hated the idea of being owned like a prize cow or something. It irked me that I couldn't make a move without Hardy now. The fact that he worked for a criminal, and that he wasn't shy about causing pain or even getting rid of people who wronged him or stood in his way, made me feel that Hardy, with his oozing charm, was evil. The devil. Or at the least, a major demon. I wanted to exorcise him from my life somehow.

"He's gotta have a weakness," I said.

"Sure," Ashton said unconvincingly. "And a couple of shlumps like us are going to find it and bring him down?" He took a long drink of his coffee and drummed his fingers on the table, watching me.

"Sounds impossible, I know. But someone like Hardy has to have hurt somebody along the line. He can't go through life pushing people around without there being someone somewhere who wants to get back at him."

"True enough, I suppose," Ashton said. "But how are we ever going to find that person? I'm no detective. Neither are you."

I stared out the window at the street. There were a lot of people out enjoying the sun and the warmth, and everyone looked happy and busy. They seemed so casual. They walked as though they had no worries, no cares, no burdens. It felt like a blues song to me and made me feel even more trapped. I scribbled a line of lyric on my napkin.

"What are you doing?" Ashton asked.

"Just scratching down a thought. This whole deal might make a good blues song."

"Like about selling your soul to the devil to be a blues giant? Robert Johnson already did that."

"Some things never go out of style," I said.

"Pain and confusion," Ashton said.

"Love and frustration," I said.

"The blues is just a good man feeling bad." We both laughed.

"Well, the thing is that at least I get to make a record. And if I make it the best I can possibly do, then maybe the music is the way out from under all of this. He can't own me forever."

"You get to be some big music hot shot, you might be able to buy him off."

"You think?"

"Ain't no percentage in thinking, brother. It's not a poor man's game," Ashton said.

"Good lyric," I said. "Who wrote that?"

"I did," he said and grinned.

It made me feel better.

CHAPTER TEN

I told Hardy to go big on a roan mare called Dizzy Flash. She came in at seventeen to one. A few days later I found a real sleeper in the third because it was raining buckets and the gelding really loved to run in the slop. There were no signs in actual races to show that, but I found great times in his workouts while the track was poor. He went off at sixty to one, and Hardy was over the moon at the results. Then, after a ten-day dry spell, I found him a last gasper. That's a horse that's almost ready for the pasture but has one last great race in him. He'd always been a come-from-behind thriller. I remembered him from his younger days and how exciting it had always been to watch him come flying from the back of the pack. Now, though, Falmouth Circuit was old. He hadn't won a race in a long, long time. He was in a race against inexperienced youngsters who had only won one or two races by the time they were four. He was listed as a forty-to-one shot.

The day dawned bright and sunny. Hardy wanted to make an event out of it and arranged to pick me up and take me to the track with him. They picked me up at noon, and we drove to the track. It was crowded, and there was a buzz you could feel in the air. The crowd was alive with it, and the tote board for the second race reflected their excitement. The odds changed every minute as bettors laid down their money on five favorites. Each of them got bet down low. Falmouth Circuit sat unchanged at forty to one for a long time. Hardy kept his eyes on me. I could feel him watching me.

"We gonna do this thing?" he asked finally. There was a rumble of anger in his voice.

"Wait," was all I said.

"Wait for what? You brought me here to play the odds and he's there. He's been there all friggin' day."

"Wait," I said again.

Hardy fumed. Jerry and Vic shrugged their huge shoulders at the same time and rocked on the balls of their feet. We were standing in the throng and leaning on the rail as I watched the tote board, and I could tell that Hardy didn't like being so visible. It was the first hint I got of him being rattled. It was three minutes to post time when the board flickered and the numbers changed. Falmouth Circuit shot up to fifty-five to one.

"Now," I said and turned and headed for the window. The three gangsters fell in behind me. We got our bets down just as the horses were at the gate.

We walked quickly up the stairs to the second balcony, where we could watch the action in the backstretch. The field had already made the first turn and were bunched tightly coming onto the straight. Our horse lagged a good ten lengths behind. The whole grandstand was in a tizzy. The favorites raced shoulder-to-shoulder, and the pace was wild. When they plunged into the third turn, Falmouth Circuit was eight lengths behind. Hardy gave me a hard look. I shrugged. He glowered.

Then the magic happened. It was like the horse found an entirely new set of gears. He closed the gap on the last horse in the pack by the middle of the turn. He was flying. Then he exploded to the outside and began passing horses like they were standing still. The announcer screamed out, "Falmouth Circuit makes a strong bid on the outside." The crowd went nuts.

He caught up to the lead horses five yards into the homestretch. There were four of them spread out in a tight row across the track. Neither gained an inch. Hardy was slamming his rolled-up form against the railing. His face was red with excitement. Everyone was in a frenzy. Time slowed to a heartbeat. The horses closed on the finish line. There was no leader. It looked like it was going to be a photo finish. Then, with scant yards to go, Falmouth Circuit kicked it up another notch. He leaped ahead by a yard, held it and flashed across the line with a narrow victory. There was bedlam around us. Hardy was leaping up and down, hugging me and punching at Jerry and Vic, who had made bets of their own.

Hardy won over fifteen thousand dollars.

"Damn, that was fun," he said on the way out of the grandstand. "Fun to watch and a lot more fun to win. But I gotta admit, you had me worried when you made me wait so long, Cree."

"I just wanted the best numbers for you."

"Well, we got that." He walked ahead of us toward the car and pulled his cell phone out of his pocket. He talked into it as he walked.

"Seems happy," I said to the goons.

"You'd be happy too if you'd loosened a noose," Vic said.

"What do you mean?"

"He owes a bunch to Solly Dario." Jerry elbowed Vic hard in the ribs, and the big man flinched and gave him a hard look. Jerry gave him a harder one back, and Vic put his head down and walked silently.

Jerry gave me the same look of stone, and I shut up. But as I watched Hardy talk on the phone, he'd lost the excitement he'd had after the win. He spoke in low tones, grave, and I could sense his seriousness. He was giving deference. He was reporting. Whoever Solly Dario was, he clearly had Hardy's utmost attention. When he closed the phone, he stepped into the car without looking at us and patted his chest pocket where the counter check was. I felt on the verge of a great discovery.

CHAPTER ELEVEN

Ashton was a whiz with the Internet. He wasn't much for games or the whole chat thing, but he could find any information that he wanted. His setup was amazing. He had three monitors hooked up to a system that was blazing fast. He showed me the community of info nerds that he belonged to. He searched out everything from the mating habits of the red kangaroo to the latest developments with the space telescope while I sat and watched. Then he typed in *Solly Dario*.

Dario was a street punk who'd worked his way up the criminal ladder with the Ricci crime family. He sat as one of their top lieutenants and also ran his own show. He'd been arrested a number of times but none of the charges had stuck. Somehow key witnesses either changed their minds about their testimony or just failed to show up for court. In his younger days, Dario had been mean and violent and fearless. Now he lived on a big country estate where he raised champion wolfhounds and was a patron of the arts who sponsored museums and libraries. He even had a foundation that awarded bursaries for inner-city kids to go to college.

But he still had his hand in the game. Ashton found references to ongoing investigations with a number of agencies focused on Dario's influence in boxing and a handful of Las Vegas casinos. He was slippery. No one had been able to pin him down on anything, and he lived unthreatened by the law. He was something of a criminal legend.

When he cross-referenced Dario with Winslow Hardy, we found an association that went back a long time. They'd been street kids together. Dario had been the one who brought Hardy to Leo Scalia. While Scalia's ventures never gained the prominence that Dario's did, the two families worked closely with the Ricci organization. And Hardy carried a lot of weight. But his weakness was that he loved to gamble. Ashton found references to a big loss in a Ricci casino that Dario had covered for him.

"That's what Vic meant," I said. "Hardy owes Dario for bailing him out of a mess with the Ricci family. That's why he wanted me in his grips so bad."

"You're the closest thing to a sure thing he's ever found," Ashton said. "Every winner that pays off for him means he can slip the bucks to Dario and take the pressure off. He needs to keep winning."

We looked at each other silently.

"You know what this means then?" I said finally.

"Yeah," Ashton said. "You get him out of debt with Dario, you might be able to walk."

"It means that I just have to keep on winning too."

"You know the odds are against that?"

"It's the only game in town, Ash."

"It's no game when you absolutely have to win."

"That old devil drives a hard bargain," I said.

"Always has," Ashton said. "Always will."

* * *

I found Blackberry Ramble by accident. I was studying another horse that had caught my interest and began to notice his name regularly in the same lines. He seemed to never be able to get beyond fourth. Judging by what the line said, he ran good races in good company but had never been able to win. "Always a bridesmaid, never a bride" was the line that best described this horse. Until now. The horse that caught my interest was called Upton, and he was a stalker. That meant that he laid off the pace in about fourth position until the homestretch and then outran horses at the very last. Blackberry Ramble ran the same kind of race. What tipped me off was the speed. The two favorites in the race liked to run wire to wire. They were pure speedsters. But this race was longer than they generally ran. It meant that stalkers like Blackberry Ramble could tuck in and let them run and then knock them off in the stretch run more easily. With the presence of Upton in the same race, it meant that my horse would likely go off at really good odds. It wasn't a sure thing, but it certainly was intriguing.

I watched Hardy's eyes light up when I told him. "Likely twenty to one by post time, you figure?" he asked.

"Yeah. Not much more."

"I'll take that any day of the week, hands down," he said.

He went in hard.

* * *

There are moments in your life that come to define you. Most times you don't even know that's what they are. They're just moments. Just living. Just what you normally do. It's only later when you look back that you discover how big they were. That's what Blackberry Ramble and the eighth race were that day. Everything stayed the same and his numbers sat right where they were supposed to. But something told me to stay off. I didn't risk any of my own money.

I didn't say a thing to Hardy. He put his money down like I'd advised. But I couldn't shake the queasy feeling in my gut. I stayed away from the track that day too. Maybe I'd grown a sixth sense. I don't know. All I know is that I didn't feel right, and I laid off. As I walked around that afternoon, the feeling of disaster kept churning in my mind.

Blackberry Ramble stumbled coming out of the gate. It took him precious long seconds to recover and get back into stride. By that time he was at the far outside of the track, and the field was charging through the first turn. He never got back into it. Didn't even come close.

The cell phone went off in my pocket. Hardy told me what happened. "It's what you can never predict," I said.

"Yeah? How much did you lose?" he asked. I could hear the rage in him.

"I didn't lay out a bet," I said.

"Oh yeah? Why's that? It was your pick."

"Gut feeling," I said.

There was a long silence. I waited. I could hear him breathing.

"We need to talk," he said. "I'm picking you up at your place. Be there."

I walked home with slow heavy steps.

CHAPTER TWELVE

The beating I took was vicious. I didn't even know it was coming because Hardy didn't say a word. They picked me up, and as soon as I sat in the backseat, Vic slammed a fist into the back of my head and I crumpled forward. I felt Jerry punch me three times in the ribs before the breath went out of me. Then Vic's big fist crashed into the back of my head again, and I blacked out.

When I came to, I was in a chair at the back of the loading dock at Hardy's warehouse. He pulled on a pair of light boxing gloves, lifted my chin with one hand and smashed a punch into my jaw with the other. Then, as Vic and Jerry held me up, he hammered me in the torso time and time again. The scariest part was the silence. None of them spoke. Hardy kept hitting me, rearing back and punching, and his face didn't change at all. It just stayed cold and hard and bitter. He beat me like a boxer beats a heavy bag. His eyes were dark pits that gave off no light. When he tired, he just waved his hand at the goons, and they let me slump back into the chair.

Hardy leaned against the wall, breathing hard through his mouth. He looked at me through the top of his eyes and sneered. "You cost me ten grand, you useless punk."

The room was spinning. I tried to open my mouth to speak, but it was full of blood. I spit it out at the floor. "Sorry" was all I could get out.

"Sorry? You leave me to carry a bad bet and all you can say is you're sorry?"

"Wasn't a bad bet. Was a good horse."

"So why did you stay out?"

"I don't know. Gut feeling, like I said."

He walked over and pushed my head back with one hand and slammed the other into my belly.

"How's that for a gut feeling, you piece of crap! Give me his hand."

Jerry lifted up my left hand and held it out. Hardy peeled the gloves off and grabbed my first two fingers and bent them back as far as they would go. He leaned forward and glared into my eyes and pushed them back farther and farther. I could feel the tendons stretch, and the pain was incredible.

"I got a gut feeling about you now too, Cree," he said. "I got a feeling maybe a one-handed blues player ain't ever gonna amount to much."

"I didn't know," I gasped.

"You knew enough to stay out without telling me. You knew enough to look out for yourself. You're a player too, Cree. You read it, but you didn't let me know. You let me take a friggin' fall. Big-time."

"I made you money."

He laughed. It was harsh and bitter-sounding. "You made me squat! You're nickel-and-diming me to nowhere. The big money I want? You ain't coming close to getting that, Wonderboy."

"I said I was sorry."

"Oh, believe me, my friend. You haven't even started being sorry."

"What do you mean?"

"What do I mean? What do I mean? I mean I friggin' own you! You, your family, your friends. I friggin' own them too. You cause me to lose, you cause them to lose. Are you getting me now, Cree? Are you?"

I leaned back in the chair and let my arms slump down. "No one else had anything to do with this."

"When you came in, they all came in. That's how it goes, schmuck."

"So what are you gonna do? None of them has any money."

"They can all feel pain."

"They're not responsible for this."

"You're responsible. Call it whatever. Guilt by association if you want."

"So what is it you want me to do?"

"I want my ten grand back. Plus I want what I should have won. You put me in a big hole here, Cree. I need out of it. Fast."

"I can't conjure up a win for you," I said and immediately regretted it.

He knelt down in front of me and looked straight into my eyes. It was his utter stillness that scared me now. I'd never seen someone stay so still, so silent, so threatening without having to move a muscle.

"You'd better. You'd better get to work and pull a friggin' rabbit out of the hat, or people are gonna start to bleed. I promise you that. You got one week."

"One week? For what, twenty thousand or so?"

"Or so," Hardy said. "Call it the upper end, closer to thirty. And that's just for starters."

"I can't do that."

"You can. And you will."

"If I can't?"

He smiled, but it was more like just pulling skin up over his teeth. There was no humor in it, no feeling. It was eerie. Haunting. Disturbing. He reached up and gripped my jaw with one hand. "If you can't, things are really going to go downhill. I don't have the time or the need to carry a bum who doesn't get me what I need. One week, Cree. One week."

He stood up and walked away. Vic and Jerry scowled at me and walked away shaking their heads. The pain I felt all through my body was nothing compared to the sheer terror I felt grip at my belly. It was a long time before I could move.

CHAPTER THIRTEEN

They say revenge is a dish best served cold. I never really got that, but I do know that I never took pain very well at all. My father was a strict churchgoing man. He had no problem with bringing out the strap whenever any of us kids would get out of line. There was always a lecture on how much we had failed him and his god. Then we were walloped, and walloped good. I remember walking away from each of those encounters with his anger and his strap feeling hot, like my skin was burning. It would take me forever to calm down. I think the reason I took to guitar and the blues so eagerly was because it gave me a place to vent. I would slam power chords. I would wrestle notes off the fret board. I would tear through twelve bars. The white-hot heat of my anger fueled my music. Without it, I wonder how much more trouble I might have gotten into. But the pain I felt from Hardy's beating had no such easy outlet.

I churned for days. While my face healed and the stiffness in my ribs and belly eased off, I felt that huge heat I'd felt as a kid. I was hip to the fact that he was too big and bad and mean for me to ever imagine taking him on physically. Plus there were Vic and Jerry to consider. So I focused my thoughts on how I could hurt him as much as he'd hurt me. I felt a bitter taste in my mouth. I felt tears burning at the back of my eyes, and I walked around my room with my fists clenched so hard my forearms ached.

There didn't seem to be any answer for my need for revenge. There didn't seem to be any easy answer for how to get out of his hold either. But I wanted both of those things more than I'd wanted anything. At that point it didn't matter to me if I lost out on the studio and his big promises of a video and connection to music biz movers and shakers. What mattered was that I got free of him. I was bluesman enough to resent the idea of being any man's slave. Finding a way out became my prime focus.

* * *

It came to me as all the best things do— unexpectedly and without stress. It just sort of fell from the sky like a great song lyric does or a fragment of melody that you hum and know in your gut that it's awesome and right. When it came to me. I sat up straight in my chair. It was a simple enough idea, but there were a ton of things that could go wrong. Still, it felt good knowing there was a road to take.

"Play both ends against the middle," I told Ashton.

"I don't get it," he said. "What does that mean exactly?"

I smiled. "It's a player's trick," I said.

"Okay. But I still don't know what it means."

"It means you put out risk on purpose to get your needs met. Like when you want a certain thing to happen, you play the win side and the lose side together so that they cancel each other out and you get the result you want anyway."

"So you put your head in the noose and hope no one kicks the chair out from under your feet?"

"Sounds about right."

"In terms of Hardy, though, what do you mean?"

"I mean I play him for the money, not the horse."

"Is this some kind of Indian thing, Cree? Because I'm really not following you at all."

I laughed, and he looked worried. We ordered ourselves another round of coffees, and after they arrived, I leaned close to him and told him the details as they had come to me. It was complicated and took a long time. When I finished, he sat back in his chair and stared out the window. Then he looked at me and nodded. But he looked a hell of a lot more worried.

CHAPTER FOURTEEN

We used Ashton's computer. When I found horses that interested me, we researched them. In a few days we learned more about bloodlines, breeding, sires, dams, thoroughbred farms, the structure of racetracks, horse anatomy, how they run and the science of racing horses than I ever thought I'd know before. Everything I knew had come from first-hand experience. But the technology gave me a university degree in understanding the math and the science behind it all. When it came to plotting odds, it sure helped. My head felt stuffed with information.

Hardy only called once.

"Time's getting short, Cree."

"I know," I said. "I'm just making sure I put you onto a sure thing."

"You'd better." He'd hung up abruptly, and Ashton gave me that grave, worried look again.

I knew that a good horse could run anywhere from eight to twelve times a season. At smaller tracks like the one we had in town, they might go more often, so we narrowed our search to include only those who looked like their owners were priming them for a climb up the ladder to major tracks. It meant they ran fewer races, but they were better contests. We also focused on horses that worked out very well and steadily but had no wins in races against good competition. We wanted speed. We wanted endurance. We wanted a late move in the final stages in the race. It meant that we wanted a router. In track talk, a router is a horse that runs routes or races of a mile or more. The sprints, those short races where blinding speed separates winners from losers, are harder to gauge and play. But routers give you more laps, more time and more room to gather information on their past efforts. So we narrowed our search to longer races and the routers that ran them.

It was important that we have a longer race to play. It was vital that we had as much information on the field of horses that would run the race we chose. It was also critical that we knew the layout of the track as closely as possible. On smaller tracks like the one we went to, the turns are sharper. It means horses on the outside aren't as far off the lead as it looks from the grandstand. It also means front-runners, horses who use their speed to get out fast and try to hold it, are less likely to put up a huge lead because they have to negotiate the turns with more care.

Ashton showed me how to research all of it. I admired him for his computer knowledge. He was impressed with my inside scoop on racing. Together we put together a "book," a list of horses with numbers we liked and that fit our preferences. In the end we whittled it down to three. When we compared the numbers, we liked our list. Then we checked the racing schedule of each of them and found that one had been raced hard very recently, and we cut our list to two. Then we headed for the track.

A horse by the numbers is just a shadow. You have to get out in the stink of the barn and the backtrack where they live and work to really see them. I had enough connections left from my days as an exercise groom to get back there with no problem.

It was an awesome world. The barns were long and low and cool. They were filled with impressive animals. When you're in the stands or watching on TV, you never really get a sense of how big and powerful a thoroughbred horse really is. To get the full-meal deal on that, you have to stand next to one. You have to touch one and feel the ripple of muscle under your palm, hear the breath huffed out like a bellows and hear the stamp of one hoof that clumps like a ton of cement on the straw bed of their stalls. You know then how powerful they are. When they look at you with those huge bottomless shining eyes, you get a feel for how smart they are, how much they know about you just from looking at you.

"Wow," Ashton said. "These guys are enormous."

"When you stand near the starting gate and they all fire off at the same time, it's like the ground explodes," I said.

"I want to do that."

"We will. As soon as we finish here."

The horse we'd come to see was named Deb's Wild Fancy. He was a big, rangy-looking chestnut gelding. When we found him, he was being led to the track for a workout. He pranced. The groom leading him was laughing as Deb's Wild Fancy literally danced sideways and then back the other way as though he were in a choreographed dance routine. He had a lot of energy. The groom turned him over to the exercise rider and came and leaned on the rail beside us. His name was Ralph, and he was eager to talk. He told us the gelding would run in three days in a mile-and-a-half race to earn a step up the ladder. The field had been chosen for him. A pack of good strong horses with good reputations, but whose finishes lacked the burst that Deb's Wild Fancy had. He was placed to win. Then he was being transported to a senior track in California where he'd run against some of the best two- and three-year-olds in the country. It was everything we wanted to hear.

Then we saw him run. It was like watching ribbon unfold time after time. He was so smooth, it looked effortless. The rider held him back with two hands. Breezing, it's called. Then, just as they passed us, the rider dropped his hands an inch with the reins, and Deb's Wild Fancy became everything the computer numbers said he was: a charging, relentless ground-eater with speed to spare. And my ticket out.

CHAPTER FIFTEEN

"So we have the horse. What do we do now?" Ashton asked. "There's no way we can influence what the odds on him will be."

"True enough," I said, looking out the window at the street from our favorite table in the coffee joint. "But we won't mess with his odds. We mess with the others."

"What do you mean?"

"I mean the form comes out the day before. Everyone who's a serious player gets it as soon as it hits the street. The line on Deb's Wild Fancy is going to show his lack of wins and fades at the finish going into a race with proven horses. He's an underdog."

"Yeah. So?"

"So we let him stay that way. Our job is to influence the other numbers and keep action off our ride."

"How do we do that?"

"Hardy," I said.

"Hardy? How is he going to help us?" Ashton looked worried, and I grinned. I was starting to get a plan on the rails. It felt good to be in the game again.

"We don't tell him that he is," I said.

"Oh, that's just great!" Ashton said, slapping the table with his palm. "The last time you didn't tell him about something almost got you killed."

"Yes. But he showed me something. Something that we needed to know."

"And what might that be?"

"Desperation," I said. "He wasn't angry that I didn't keep him in the play.

He was hot because he lost—and he can't afford to lose."

"So?"

"So we put him on a different horse."

He gave me a look of utter disbelief.

"You want to get him to put money down on a horse that you know isn't going to do anything? How is that going to help?

"When there's a sudden drop of loot, it shows on the odds board right away. The amount in the win pool goes up, and the odds go down. Every player worth his salt watches how the pool is being affected. It tells them where the action is."

He thought for a moment.

"So you get Hardy to lay down a bundle on this other horse. That makes the players react and the odds change. So the numbers on our horse go up?"

"You're a born handicapper, kid." I grinned.

"I just want to live to see thirty," he said. "Hanging with you sometimes makes that feel like a challenge."

"Yeah, well, it's all about the road and not the map, baby."

"Cool enough," he said and clapped me on the shoulder. "But maybe we can try truckin' down something other than a dirt road sometime there, Lightnin'." He laughed. I felt good. Ashton was a great friend.

* * *

The thing about horse players is that the smarter they get, the less they really know. Numbers are like a complicated chord progression. You can stare at them all you like, but you actually have to put your hand on the guitar to make any sense of it. Horse players sit back and watch numbers and never do anything to work with them. They come to believe that the numbers have a mind of their own and will fall into the pattern they're supposed to, and that their job is to watch them and react when all the signs are clear. This is what I was counting on.

The other thing that I was counting on is what players dread the most. The unseen. The weird little things that go on in the background that affect the way things turn out. A bandage or a tape job on a fetlock or a knee. A sheen of liniment on the shoulder or the haunch. Blinkers over the eyes or tape on the ears. Or just the sudden appearance of numbers in a cold hard splash that drives them to the windows in droves. Horse players are a superstitious bunch. They're certain that the Fates are lined up to pick their pockets, and the things they can't control or understand send them into hard mental tailspins. I needed that to happen. I needed Hardy for that.

The other thing I needed was money to play. A lot of it. When the big moment came,

I needed to be at the window with a pailful.
I knew the only place I could turn for that.
But the thing I needed most desperately
was one of those things I couldn't control.
I could get Hardy to believe he was riding
the next sure thing. I could have a plan for
play money. What I couldn't control was
the weather the day of the race, a sudden
accident in the exercise ring, a horse in the
field juiced on speed, a spill during the race,
an injury or the sudden pulling of my horse
at the gate. There were more than enough
imagined pitfalls. I could only take care of
the things I could control. I left Ashton at
the coffee joint and went to do just that.

CHAPTER SIXTEEN

Race day dawned like a minor miracle. There wasn't a cloud in the sky and not even a hint of a breeze. It was warm. The whole day smelled like roses. If there were such a thing as an omen, then I guess the day breaking open like that was it for me. I called Ashton, and we arranged to meet at the coffee shop and then go for breakfast. I showered and headed out. But Vic and Jerry were waiting for me on the porch. They stood there mute as statues. I couldn't see their eyes behind their mirrored shades. All Vic did was extend an arm and indicate that I should walk ahead of them to the limo that sat at the curb, its tinted windows giving no hint as to who was inside. Jerry reached around me and opened the back door. I looked inside. Hardy was sitting there with Ashton, who looked pale and very nervous.

"What's this?" I asked.

"Insurance," Hardy said and smiled.

"Against what?"

"Me gettin' the friggin' blues, Cree."

"I got you on a good horse."

"That's what buddy boy is here to ensure. The boys will sit on him until we see what goes down."

"I'm telling you what's going to go down is that you're walking away with a ton of cash today."

He laughed. It was a cold laugh, empty of any feeling. It sent a chill down my spine.

"Words. That's all that is. Words. Until I see something concrete, your buddy the nerd gets babysat. If the outcome is good, the outcome is good. If it isn't...well, use your imagination. What's this magic horse's name anyway?"

"Regal Splendor. He's a six-to-one shot in the second."

"You want me to go big on a six-to-one shot?"

"No. I want you in on the next sure thing. It's what you asked."

"Regal Splendor. Sounds like...whattaya call it...a good sign."

"It is."

I looked at Ashton. He shrugged and looked at the floor. Jerry put a big wide hand in the middle of my back and pushed me into the car. I sat on the jump seat facing Hardy. He sat back and smoothed his clothes and grinned humorlessly. We pulled into traffic. Vic and Jerry eased in behind us in the suv. I coughed nervously, and Hardy's cold stare froze me to the seat.

He eased his jacket back and showed me the butt of an automatic pistol. Then he closed it and patted the small bulge where it sat in the holster under his armpit.

"Ah, a day at the races. So stylish. So fun. Don't you think, there, nerd?"

He jostled Ashton in the ribs with his elbow. My friend just continued to stare at the floor. We drove to the track in silence. Hardy leaned back in the seat staring at me, eyes as empty as any I had ever seen. Just at that moment, the plan I had concocted offered me little comfort.

* * *

We killed time until the races started by cruising through the barns. Hardy was his most charming self. He scored a lot of points with handlers and grooms with his jokes and the roll of bills he showed buying coffees for them all. When he asked a few people about how Regal Splendor looked, he got nothing but strong opinions about his chances. A long shot, but a horse that would definitely be in the race even if it was the favorites that would rule the day. He seemed pleased with that.

"Did your homework," he said to me as we walked back to the grandstand.

"It's what you asked," I said.

"How long do I wait before I put the bet down?"

"I'd wait until the end of the first race." Deb's Wild Fancy was in the second too. "Don't want to go too soon and tip your hand. But you also don't want to wait too long either," I said.

"Are you in on this one this time?"

"You bet," I said, and he grinned.

* * *

Hardy won fifteen hundred dollars in the first race on a horse I picked out of the post parade. She just looked good.

He came back from the window with a gleam in his eye.

"If that's how this is going to go today, you and the nerd will be doing whatever it is nerds do at night."

I only nodded. The numbers on the tote board read exactly as I wanted them to. Regal Splendor moved up to eight to one, and there wasn't a move on Deb's Wild Fancy at all. He stayed at thirty to one. Hardy watched me read the board. I could feel his tension rising. When the numbers flashed across in an update with twelve minutes to go, I saw that they had stayed the same. "Time to go," I said.

"Everything good?"

"Everything's perfect." I stood and followed him to the window. I was counting on long lines that would let me slip into a separate one from Hardy. My luck held. He only glanced at me. I shrugged and pointed to the number of people ahead of him. He nodded. I waited for him by the stairs. He had the assured glow that bettors have when they know they're on a sure thing. He was actually smiling. He clapped me soundly on the back, and we walked back to our seats. The crowd was buzzing. There were three horses bet down to almost identical odds. Then, thirty seconds before post time, the numbers flashed in the final update and Regal Splendor sat at ten to one. Hardy's smile got even bigger.

"How big did you go?" I asked.

"I went ten large."

"Nice payout." I said.

"It will be," he said. Then he looked at me sternly. "Won't it, Cree?"

"I told you, there's a ton of cash to be won on this race."

The track announcer said the fateful words, "And they're at the post." The crowd hushed, and I could feel the pulse of adrenaline everywhere. Hardy's legs bumped up and down, and his hands tapped the top of his thighs. The gate flew open and they were off.

CHAPTER SEVENTEEN

I t went just as I thought it would. The three favorites controlled the race. They went to the front and challenged the rest of the field to stay with them. Regal Splendor ran fourth with a two-length gap between him and the favorites. Deb's Wild Fancy hung back in seventh position and ran evenly without attracting any notice from either the crowd or the other jockeys. The pace was frantic. There wasn't a nose between the three leaders, and the crowd was wild. Regal Splendor made a small move coming into the final turn and moved just behind them. Hardy jumped up and down in place beside me. I couldn't hear myself think for the noise all around us. There'd been plenty of money bet, and people were going crazy.

Then, as they rounded the turn into the homestretch, Deb's Wild Fancy came charging out of nowhere. He blasted into the straight. Regal Splendor had moved into a small lead, but the leaders were still in a tight pack. Deb's Wild Fancy had to run wide, but he had a ton of gas left and his stride stretched out. He galloped hard to pull even as the crowd noise became enormous. Then it was between him and Regal Splendor. I don't think I breathed. Hardy was bashing me on the shoulder and his face was crazed and wild and he yelled things that didn't even sound like words to me. Then with ten yards to go, Deb's Wild Fancy eased ahead and won going away by three-quarters of a length.

Hardy slumped down into his seat. The crowd was electrified by the race, and the hubbub was tremendous. I sat down quietly beside Hardy.

"Let me see your ticket," he said.

I handed it to him. He looked at it briefly. He nodded. He scowled. Then he tucked it into his pocket and elbowed me hard to my feet and put his hand inside his jacket. "Walk," was all he said.

He walked behind me all the way to the parking lot. He didn't say a word to me, but he didn't have to. The same unnerving quiet that had settled over him during my beating spoke volumes to me as we walked. Some people carry the threat of themselves like a cloud, and Hardy's roiled all around me. When we got to the car, he raised his hand and Vic and Jerry pulled up the black Navigator with Ashton inside.

"What's to it, boss?" Vic asked.

"He played me," Hardy said. "We'll settle up at the warehouse."

Jerry got out of the Navigator and grabbed me by the elbow. Hard. Then he pushed me into the backseat, and I slammed into Ashton with such force that our heads banged together. Vic drove fast following Hardy, and neither of them spoke. Ashton and I could only glance at each other, but I could tell that he was worried. I was beyond that. The ticket Hardy grabbed from me had been a thousand-dollar ticket. It was a big win. But it wasn't going to be enough.

Vic and Jerry manhandled us through the loading dock and into the warehouse. Hardy had gotten there moments before. There were no employees left in the building. It was deathly quiet. While Vic stood in front of us, Jerry placed a pair of chairs in the middle of the floor on a large sheet of heavy plastic.

"What's that for?" Ashton asked.

"Makes cleanup easier," Vic said and grinned.

"Cleanup of what?" he asked.

"You," Vic said.

Hardy came down the stairs from his office. He'd changed into a jogging suit and black leather gloves. He was carrying a hammer and a chisel. He walked past his henchmen without a word and separated the chairs so that they sat facing each other. Then he motioned for Vic and Jerry to bring us over. They shoved us so hard that we stumbled and crashed into each other, and Ashton sprawled on the plastic. Vic kicked him and hauled him to his feet. Jerry slapped me on the back of the head and I fell into a chair, nearly tipping over before I planted my feet and settled. Hardy stood in front of us tapping the head of the hammer on the chisel.

"Do you know what you cost me, Cree?" he asked.

"Ten large?" I asked.

"More than that, buddy boy. I needed this race. I needed the win. You have no idea how badly."

"Actually, I do." I said.

"You do?"

"Yeah. Your goons let it slip that you owe a lot of money to Solly Dario."

He flashed a look at Vic and Jerry, who shrugged and looked away. I could see him grip the tools tighter in his fist. "Yeah, well, none of that matters now. What matters is that you played me. You took my trust and my ten grand and set me back. Again. Bigger. With more consequences. And I got to even up now."

He stepped up to Ashton, and Vic moved in to press him into his seat by pushing down on his shoulders. Hardy knelt and held the edge of the chisel just below his kneecap. "You ever seen a sculpture being made, Cree?"

"No," I said, barely above a whisper.

"Messy. Bits of stuff flying all over. But before I start, I just want to ask you one question."

"What's that?" I asked.

"Who fronted you the grand to lay down on the horse?"

"I did." The voice came from the door of the loading dock, and the three gangsters spun around to see who spoke.

"Solly," Hardy said. The tools dropped onto the plastic.

Solly Dario and four of his men strode into the warehouse. They were all business. Vic and Jerry stepped back away from us. Solly stepped up to Hardy and stood mere inches away, staring at him sternly. "Come to collect," he said.

"I ain't got it, Solly. I woulda. But the kid played me."

"Oh, I'm not here to collect from you, Winslow. I'm here to collect from Cree."

Hardy looked at me and just stared with his mouth hanging wide open.

CHAPTER EIGHTEEN

"**Y**ou got a good kid here, Winslow. Be a shame to see you put him out of commission." Solly began peeling off his gloves finger by finger and eyeing Hardy all the while. Ashton and I watched and waited.

"He don't play straight, Solly," Hardy said. "He's got no code."

"Fact is, he does."

"Whattaya mean?"

Dario finished removing his gloves, folded them gently and laid them in the pocket of his overcoat.

"He's got a code and he's got moxie. He come to me. Told my boys you sent him, and he told me about your issue."

"My issue?" Hardy put a hand against his chest and bowed slightly.

"You gave the kid a week to come up with the juice you still owe me. That's a big load to throw off on a young kid. Especially one who has such a good high end as this kid does."

"Solly, I was just taking care of your end."

"My end takes care of itself, Winslow. Always has, always will. Like this kid walkin' through my door. Good things just come to me." Solly looked at them, and his four boys all grinned. "So he tells me about his gig with you. Then he tells me how he needs a hand to get this done. So I listen like any good businessman would. Turns out he wants to teach you something, and me, I figure that's a good thing on accounta you being into me for so much means you could use a lesson in how things work."

"I don't get it," Hardy said.

Dario patted him on the cheek.

"I know you don't. The kid needed someone to front the cash for a big roll out on this horse. Said if I did, he would earn me back the vig and the juice from you and a whole lot more."

"I still don't get it," Hardy said.

"And that's why you'll never be a good businessman, Winslow. See, the kid knew the horse would win, but he needed someone to take the attention off him at the last minute. Hence your ten large.

"You dumped this big wager, and it shows up in the win pool. That gets every player in the joint drooling, and they lay out more and no one touches the money horse. In fact, his odds go up. When that happens, I lay down my wager at the very last minute, and next thing you know,

I'm collecting big. Big. And the thing is, the kid would only do it if your debt was cleared with the winnings."

"He still played me for the sap," Hardy said.

"Get over yourself, Winslow. The kid knew you could handle the ten grand. You were only sweating what you owed me. You were the means to the end, and if he played you, he did it perfectly. Perfectly. Kinda like he plays the blues."

"You heard him?"

"Naturally. I said he had a good high end. Kid's gonna make a big splash, and I'm in the front door."

"So I owe you nothing?"

"That's right. Free and clear. Just like the kid and his pal here."

"But he still belongs to me, right? He still plays the track for me?"

"Winslow, you don't hear so good sometimes. I said free and clear. Along with clearing your debt, he cleared himself too. That means his family, all the connections to him you got too. Granted, every now and then he's going to do me a favor when a sure thing comes up, and maybe I'll let you in on that action when it happens. Then again, maybe I won't."

"So what's the lesson I'm supposed to learn here?" Hardy asked. He looked beat.

"Tell him, Cree." Dario grinned.

Hardy looked at me. "There is only ever really one sure thing," I said.

"Oh, yeah," Hardy said coldly. "And what might that be?"

"You have to make your own luck, because there's never really a next sure thing."

"Still talking in song lyrics, aren't you?" Hardy asked.

As it turned out, I was.

EPILOGUE

We finished recording my first CD within a month. It was called *Sure Thing Blues*, and the critics hailed it for the force of its guitar work and its intelligent lyrics. By the end of that summer, it was the number-one blues recording in the country and I had three prime videos and a major concert tour opening for Buddy Guy. Ashton became my manager. He put together one of the hottest bands on the planet to back me up, and we worked the crowds like rock and rollers. We were a hit. My father came to one of our gigs.

When he came to the dressing room after, there were tears in his eyes.

"I never knew," he said.

"Never knew what, Dad?" I asked.

He grabbed me into the first real big hug I remember getting from him and held me tight for a long time. "Never knew the many ways we can be blessed. You've been blessed with incredible music, and I've been blessed with a musician and a son."

We've been real tight ever since.

Hardy faded away, and even though I caught sight of him the few times I ventured to the track, he pretended not to see me. That was fine with me. Solly Dario financed the CD, the video and the equipment, and the buses and the trucks we needed to tour, but was content to be a silent partner. No one ever knew about our connection. Still, when there were good numbers in the racing form I let him know. I don't know if he ever made the bets, and I don't care. What mattered was that I was on my way to becoming the next great bluesman. I settled into the life of writing and playing and chasing my star across the heavens that had opened up for me.

Oh, and what Hardy said about talking in song lyrics? He was right. The first single from my debut album was called "The Next Sure Thing."

You can make your money in the fields all day,
Or you can make your money in a different
*   way,*
But you gotta get up and show your pluck,
Because winners are the ones who make
*   their own kind of luck.*
There's winners and there's losers, and
*   here's the thing:*
You can waste a lot of time waitin' on the
*   next sure thing.*

RICHARD WAGAMESE is one of Canada's foremost Native authors and journalists. In a career spanning thirty-two years, he has worked in newspapers, radio, television and publishing, and has won numerous awards for his work. Awarded an Honorary Doctor of Letters degree from Thompson Rivers University in 2010, he lives outside of Kamloops, British Columbia, with his wife and Molly the Story Dog.

Titles in the Series

 **RAPID READS**